THE PRINCESS OF ZILZILAM

TAHIR SHAH

MAEDEH TAJAFARY

THE PRINCESS OF ZILZILAM

A Teaching Story

TAHIR SHAH

MAEDEH TAJAFARY

MMXXIV

Secretum Mundi Publishing Ltd
124 City Road
London
EC1V 2NX
United Kingdom

www.secretum-mundi.com
info@secretum-mundi.com

First published by Secretum Mundi Publishing Ltd, 2024
A version of this story originally appeared in *Scorpion Soup* by Tahir Shah, 2013

THE PRINCESS OF ZILZILAM

© TAHIR SHAH

Artwork drawn by Maedeh Tajafary

Tahir Shah asserts the right to be identified as the Author of the Work
in accordance with the Copyright, Designs and Patents Act 1988.

A CIP catalogue record for this title is available from the British Library.

ISBN 978-1-915876-05-8

VERSION 31012024

Visit the author's website:
Tahirshah.com

All rights reserved. No part of this publication may be reproduced, stored in a retrieval system, or transmitted, in any form or by any means, electronic, mechanical, photocopying, recording or otherwise, without the prior written permission of the publisher.

This book is sold subject to the condition that it shall not, by way of trade or otherwise, be lent, re-sold, hired out or otherwise circulated without the publisher's prior consent in any form of binding or cover other than that in which it is published and without a similar condition including this condition being imposed on the subsequent purchaser.

Shiraz lies to the east, so travel west to find it,
and be ripened by adventure.

Persian saying

Teaching Stories

When I was small, I was told stories from morning till night.

I was told stories about genies and witches and about great birds that could carry away elephants on their wings… and stories about distant kingdoms and magical lands ruled by warrior kings.

I was told stories of good and bad… stories of hope and others of despair.

I was even told stories about stories.

And all the while, I listened, amazed.

The more I listened, the more my mind worked… and the more I came to understand that these stories had a power about them, a secret lifeblood all of their own.

They were magical instruments, machineries that could alter states of mind and change the way we think.

But most importantly of all, stories can teach us, without us realizing that they are doing so at all.

Part of the default programming of man, stories are within us all.

Born into us, they make us who we are – they make us human.

Since earliest childhood, I have feasted on stories as a way of learning about the world, and learning about myself. They have been my dictionary and my encyclopaedia, my classroom, my guide, and my very best friend.

To descend down through the layers of stories is to be reborn, into a dominion of fantasy – one touched by real magic.

Pre-eminent within the great treasuries of tales, it is teaching stories like this one that have shown me the path to follow beyond the next horizon, and have made me the man I am.

Tahir Shah

There was once a green jinn who, tricked by a magician, had lain trapped inside a battered lead urn for a thousand years and a day.

As he languished there, the jinn vowed that he would wreak havoc on mankind if he were ever to get free.

He waited. And he waited.

And he vowed and he vowed.

But the urn in which the jinn was imprisoned
had been hurled by the magician into the
deepest stretch of the Red Sea.

And there it lay for an eternity.

Until, one dark night, it was moved by a rogue current, and then swept up in a fisherman's net as it raked across the sea floor.

The net was hauled up onto the decks,
and the urn was discovered.

Hopeful of finding treasure, the captain wasted no time in breaking the lead seal.

Within an instant, the green jinn had surged from the container, slain the captain and his men, and sucked out all the blood in their veins.

Soaring up and up into the night, his form billowed outwards and upwards, until he became the sky and the heavens.

'I vow to slaughter every living thing on this earth!' he declared. 'And shall not rest until every heart – human or animal – has been extinguished, and until I have devoured every last drop of blood!'

With that, the green jinn opened his mouth and bore down on the city of Alexandria.

Believing that an eclipse was taking place, the people ran into the twisting streets of the old city and gazed up at the sky.

What they saw in its place was more terrifying than any far-fetched nightmare.

A kaleidoscope of carnage, the green jinn's
mouth was leering down towards them:
fifty rows of blood-stained teeth; the rotting,
festering cadavers of unknown dead.

Disease.

The putrefying stench of death.

Blood, blood, blood.

The people of Alexandria charged about in all directions, fleeing for their lives.

Some hid under their beds.
Others dived into empty barrels.
More still threw themselves into the sea.

Standing in the middle of the main street
was a young man called Adam.

Unlike the other people panicking
around him, he was not fearful.
Rather, he was intrigued.

A fraction of a second before the jinn's mouth claimed its prey, Adam raised an index finger high above his head and called out:

'Whatever depraved creature you are, desist for a moment, until you have heard what I have to say! Not to allow me to speak would be an act of despicable cowardice!'

It just so happened that the green jinn was troubled by almost nothing at all, but the thought of being regarded as a coward vexed him greatly.

So he paused, his mouth in mid-attack,
his eyes rolling with rage.
'How could you consume us,' bawled Adam
as loudly as he was able, 'without informing
us why you are doing so?'

The green jinn shook with ire.
And as he shook, the heavens shook,
and the world shook as well.

'Your pitiable race entrapped me in an urn for a thousand years and a day,' he roared, 'and you, and all other living things, are simply paying the price of my wrath!'

With the people of the city hastening
about in terror around him, Adam
touched a fingertip to his chin.
Thinking for a moment, he uttered:
'Well, O mighty creature, surely you would
wish to talk to me before you snuff out my life.'

The jinn drew breath to speak. As he did so, the palm trees on the coast were sucked back, as if a tempest was about to make landfall. 'I have no time to waste in meeting my victims one by one!' he spat.

But before the monster could utter another syllable, Adam held up his finger again. ‘I feel embarrassed to tell you this,’ he said slowly, ‘but in the lanes of the old city everyone’s gossiping about you.’

‘No doubt they are declaring how
fearsome I am!’ cried the monster.
‘Alas, they are not, O great one,’
Adam replied.

The jinn narrowed his eyes,
each one the size of the moon.
'I shall slay you first for uttering lies!'

Adam held his ground, his head cocked back as he took in the creature's immense, billowing form.

'They are saying that you're attacking us out of fear,' he said, 'and out of sheer cowardice. They say that you couldn't harm an ant, let alone a great city such as Alexandria!'

'*Pah*!' exclaimed the green jinn. 'I could swallow the entire city whole! And I will!' Swelling in size until even larger than before, the monster bore down once again.

But Adam laughed at the sight.
'Your cowardice is surely proven by your size,'
he said. 'Any creature so enormous could
destroy an entire city. The challenge would be
to cause the same harm when smaller in scale.'

The green jinn emitted a crazed shriek of fury. So loud and violent was it that the ground buckled as though struck by an earthquake. 'I could slay you all if I were half the size!' he boasted, before instantly reducing his form to the size of a mountain.

Adam held up a thumb.
'You are still very big,' he said, 'and it is making conversing with you challenging. Could you not make yourself a little smaller?'

The green jinn shrank again, from the size of a mountain until he was the height of a giant – a giant in human form. His mouth packed with sharp yellow teeth, each one framed in red, he loomed down over Adam.

'Speak your last words, O mortal!' he bellowed.

Once again, Adam touched
a finger to his chin.
'Surely even a giant could exact terrible damage on a place like this,' he said. 'But that's not what the people of Alexandria think. As I told you, they say that you couldn't harm an ant!'

The green jinn turned purple with wrath,
his mouth dripping with blood.
'Show me an ant, and I shall smite it!'
he exclaimed.

Adam leant down and pretended
to pick a speck from the ground.
'Here is an ant,' he said.

Filling his lungs with air, the jinn was about to blow a jet of fire down at the ant when Adam said:

'As everyone knows, the people of Alexandria are remarkably hard to impress. They take any opportunity to make fun of people from outside the city. And if they see a giant killing an ant – well, that's not going to impress them at all.'

The green jinn released his breath.

He frowned.
'Well, what *would* impress them?' he asked.
'And tell me swiftly, or I'll snuff you out
as soon as look at you.'

Adam paused to think, and then replied: 'Well, surely, what would impress them would be an ant to be dispatched by something even smaller than it, like a flea.'

The green jinn spat blood.
'I have my dignity to think of, you know!'
he exclaimed. 'I am a great jinn, and am
not going to transform myself into a flea.'

‘A pity,’ answered Adam. ‘Then the people will gossip about you all the more.’

'But I am just about to kill every last one of them!' bawled the green jinn. 'So I really don't care what they say!'

Adam sighed.
'But surely as a creature of such dignity and poise, you would feel all the more satisfied were you to prove your strength by such an insignificant act as killing an ant.'

Spitting blood and then fire,
the green jinn reduced his size from
that of a giant to that of a flea.
'Show me the ant,' said a faint voice,
'so that I may smite it at once!'

But the young man wasn't listening.

Instead, he stepped forwards and ground the sole of his sandal into the dirt, until the green jinn was quite definitely dead.

Word of Adam's bravery and cunning spread through Alexandria, and Adam was hailed as the city's saviour. Gifts and titles were lavished upon him, and the wealthiest members of society sought to marry him to their most beautiful daughters.

But, courteously, Adam refused all the awards, the gifts, and the invitations to wed. Packing a simple leather satchel, he set out into the desert, hoping to have time and space to think.

With the stars glinting in the heavens above, he sat beside his campfire. Staring into the flames, his mind thought about the frailty of jinns and of men.

Suddenly, the young man heard a voice. 'Adam, dear Adam,' it said. 'My name is Leila, and I am the daughter of the King of Zilzilam. I am trapped beneath the very sands on which you are camped. Rescue me and I promise to fill your heart with joy.'

Adam twisted round to the left,
then the right, but the enveloping
darkness was empty of any life.
'I can't see you,' Adam whispered.
'Am I imagining you?'

The voice came again, a little louder than before, running on the breeze. 'I am trapped beneath the sands. Walk ten paces south of the fire. Dig down with your hands and you will find a stone slab. Pull it back and descend.'

Wondering whether he was dreaming, Adam glanced back at the fire. The embers were glowing now, fanned by the wind.

He was about to curl up on his blanket and sleep, but the voice came a third time: 'Please come and save me, I beg you...'

Adam got to his feet and counted ten paces south of the campfire. Then, kneeling, he dug down through the cool sand with his hands. He was about to give up when his fingertips touched something hard.

Stone.

Digging faster, he unearthed a granite slab, a great iron ring set squarely in the middle. Without giving it any thought, he yanked the ring with all his strength, and the slab slid easily away.

Adam peered down the hole into a dawn realm. Squinting, he made out a kind of tropical jungle: a profusion of trees and luxuriant vines, insects and suffocating heat.

Climbing down through the boughs of a colossal tree, he made his way onto the forest floor.

As he stood there, taking in a scene from a dreamscape, first light broke through.

A pair of suns rose both at once
– one in the east, the other in the west.
Shading his eyes, Adam watched as the
jungle came to life.

Animals he had never seen before swung from one vine to the next, or prowled between the trees, hunting their morning prey.

There were sloths with two heads,
zebras in rainbow stripes, and cheetahs
weighed down with mighty ibex horns.
And there were giant anteaters as well,
and mice with human-like hands and feet,
and spiders the size of antelopes.

The voice wafted
through the jungle once again:
'Clear your mind of everything you know,
Adam,' it cautioned, 'and place one foot
before the other. Whatever you do, do not
glance down at your feet.'

How do I know that I can trust you? Adam thought.
Reading his mind, the voice answered:
'You do not, and that's why you can.'

Doing as he was instructed, Adam trod
a path through the trees, taking care
not to look down.

As he paced along, he smelled the aroma of roasting meat and the tart scent of bitter oranges. After that he felt a strange sensation… a sensation of something crawling over his feet and legs.

Straining to obey the voice, he forced himself to refrain from looking down. But the smell and the tingling became too great. Unable to withstand a moment more, Adam lowered his gaze.

Horror is too feeble a word to describe his distress. His feet and legs were sheathed in worms, glowing red as they gnawed at his flesh. As they did so, they emitted a coating of waxy oil – a kind of anaesthetic.

Fearfully, Adam swished the worms away. But as he did so, more appeared, until his hands were covered in them as well.

As he fought in a frenzy to rid himself of the scourge, the voice came once again. Soothing and calm, it drifted effortlessly through the trees.

'Rip off your shirt,' it said, 'and allow
the worms to feast on your chest.'
'But they're killing me!'
Adam shouted out loud.

'Trust me,' said the voice.

Without any other choice, Adam tore off his shirt. The worms slithered all over his chest, glowing red as they got to work on it.

Quite suddenly, they began to turn purply blue and fall away as scabs.

Adam tramped on through the suffocation of trees, following the voice. The undergrowth became increasingly dense, until it was a struggle to make any headway at all.

Progressing inch by inch, Adam began to sense grave danger. Something deep inside was cautioning him to turn back, to flee. But, as before, the voice soothed him, luring him forwards.

All of a sudden, the trees gave way to a wide clearing, the ground infested with orange beetles armed with crab claws.

In the middle of the glade was a primitive machine. The sides consisted of three pairs of multiple scimitars, each one attached to a flywheel. The central unit was a mass of cogs and levers with a large pair of scales at the front. But the base of the creation was not mechanical at all.

It was alive.

Scaly and avocado green, it was the colour and consistency of an alligator's back, and it was moving slowly, as if rearranging itself.

Approaching cautiously, crunching a path through the orange beetles, Adam took in the details of the outlandish contraption. As he drew close, he noticed something – something that caused his feet to root themselves to the ground.

A woman was encased
in the mechanical abdomen.

Strapped down, she was unable to move.
The scimitars were angled in such a way
as to carve her up if she tried to escape.

Without being informed, Adam understood
the woman was Princess Leila.
'I shall disarm this *thing* and release you!'
he exclaimed, quite overcome with sorrow.

The princess did not reply. Not at first.
She just blinked, the rest of her
body held rigid.

Then, telepathically, she said:
'Dear Adam, I'm indebted for your bravery.
But there is only one way to rescue me. In the
pans of the scales you will need to place two
objects. The first is Hope, and the other, Fear.
Attempt to disentangle me and I shall be
chopped to the finest mincemeat.'

‘But Hope and Fear have no form,’
Adam said. ‘They are invisible, intangible.’

The princess blinked once again.
'It is for you to find them,' she replied,
tears running down her cheek.
'Where shall I search?'
'In your heart.'

Adam reached forwards until his hand was no
more than an inch from the machine.
He could feel the princess's warmth.
'I will save you,' he said, 'if I have to scour
the universe for Hope and for Fear…'

With that, he was gone.

Retracing his path to the surface, Adam found himself at the campfire, the embers still crackling and spitting in the breeze.

Leaned back on his haunches,
he pondered how and where to find
the qualities needed for the scales.
'I shall set out at dawn and travel the world,'
he whispered, 'and will not give up until
I have captured Hope and Fear.'

Before the sun had risen over the horizon,
Adam's footsteps stretched in a line to eternity.

He walked through days and nights, seeking out anyone who could help him with his quest.

In the next kingdom, he met a hermit who listened to his tale. When he had heard it, the recluse instructed him to search out the Blue Mountains. Only there, the hermit insisted, could the riddle be solved.

At the Blue Mountains, Adam was informed by a diviner that the only way to find Fear and Hope was not to search for them at all.

Undeterred, he kept going on his quest.

He walked and he walked, and he walked and he walked, until he had crossed half the known world. Each person he asked pointed him in the direction of another, until he was despondent and almost broken.

Health suffering from worry, he realized how deeply he had fallen in love with Princess Leila.

After months of adventure, he found himself in the middle of nowhere – at the same desert campfire where his journey had begun.

'I have failed you, dearest Leila,' he said in a whisper, his words carried away on the breeze.

'No, no, you have not, Adam,' came the voice. 'Look into your heart and you'll know what to place on the scales.'

Plunging his head in his hands,
he struggled to reach a decision.
But he could not.

And so, unable to carry on, he paced over to the stone slab and descended back into the jungle world in which the King of Zilzilam's daughter was kept prisoner.

Although months and years had passed on the surface, it seemed as if the sands of the hourglass fell far more slowly in the jungle realm than they did above.

Indeed, hardly a day had gone by since he had embarked on his quest.

Wending his way through the trees, Adam retraced his path towards the glade in which the princess was imprisoned. As he walked fitfully between the vines, he noticed a mango tree, the ripe fruit hanging down in great quantities.

Overcome with hunger,
he picked one of the mangoes and ate it.

Within a few feet of the tree, he reached the glade in which the machine was still standing. As before, the scimitars were razor sharp, glinting in the blinding light.

While he watched, they began to move as if his arrival had triggered them. The scimitars scythed alarmingly through the air and, as they did so, the machine's reptilian underbelly coursed back and forth, surging to life.

'Please hurry!' whispered the princess.
'Precious time is running out. In moments,
I fear I shall expire!'

Adam stood before the machine, his blood fortified with adrenalin. Although desperate to rescue the princess, he felt helpless. With her death a moment away, Adam knew he had to try something.

As he conjured up the courage to overcome his fear and destroy the machine, he felt his face and hands running with perspiration.

Fear, he thought, wiping his forehead dry.
This is Fear!

Rinsing a hand over his brow, he collected
a few drops of sweat and dripped them
into the left pan of the scale.
But what about Hope?

Drawing a deep breath, Adam was about to resign himself to failure when he remembered the mango seed still clutched in his hand.

'*This* is Hope,' he said. 'The Hope of a mango tree's future.'

In a quick movement, he dropped the seed into the second pan. The machine whirred and grunted, the scimitars flashing in the jungle light.

All of a sudden, the straps and bindings disintegrated. Princess Leila was free.

Adam and the princess returned to the surface, and to the Land of Zilzilam.

Forty days of celebration were held, so overjoyed was Leila's father that his favourite daughter had been saved.

When the festivities were at an end,
Adam and the princess were wed in
a tumultuous marriage ceremony.

Another forty days of festivities followed.

With time, Adam ascended to the throne of Zilzilam, reigning as its king for many years. His wisdom and courage are still spoken of today, and his acts of kindness are the stuff of legend far beyond the ancient walls of Zilzilam.

As the years passed, King Adam devoted more and more of his time to improving the kingdom and the living standards of its people.

He ensured everyone had enough food and a good education, and that every citizen had the opportunity to come to him directly with their problems. The gates to the palace were always open and everyone knew that the wise king would see them if they needed his help.

One evening, when he had ruled for seventeen years, Adam was sitting in the durbar attending to some official papers.

As he pressed his signet ring into a wax seal, a wizened old man staggered in. The man had a long white beard that reached down to his knees and was wearing a jet-black cloak that covered his form entirely.

Rising from his throne, King Adam
went to greet the stranger.

When they were both seated, and once tea had been served, the old man spoke: 'O great King Adam of Zilzilam,' he said, his words muffled with age, 'I have waited seventy years to bring you a message, a message destined to save your kingdom and your life.'

Adam looked into the old man's dull eyes and wondered whether he was unhinged. But before he could say a word, the stranger went on:

‘When I was a young man,’ he said, ‘I was a shepherd on a remote hillside a great distance from here. From dawn until dusk each day, I tended the family flocks. And each night, I would bed down on the hay in a little stone barn and I would sleep like the dead.

'One night, while deep asleep, I walked from the barn, over the hills, until I came to a jagged rock face. There, in a cleft between the crags, an oracle spoke to me. It said that I was to be a messenger and that one day many years hence, a good king would be saved by the message I was to impart.'

‘What was the message?’ asked Adam gently.
The old man held out a withered hand.
‘I shall tell you,’ he said.

'Each night I would return to the crag as a dream-walker. And I would listen to the message of the oracle. Little by little, the oracle passed on details of the message in a most unusual way. Only when the entire message had been entrusted to me did I awake to understand that I had been the confidant to an oracle.

'As the messenger, I was instructed to keep the message with me at all times in a certain way, and to bring it to you on this precise day. The oracle said that you, King Adam, would understand the secret wisdom held within it, and that by doing so, your kingdom would endure until eternity.'

‘Could I have the message?’
Adam asked, growing a little impatient.
Again, the old man held out a hand.
‘I shall give it to you,’ he said solemnly.

Standing slowly to his feet, he unfastened the buttons of his jet-black cloak and the robe fell to the floor. Beneath it, the ancient was naked.

Every inch of his skin was tattooed with words.
'*This* is the message,' he said.

And with that, he expired.

Bending over the emaciated corpse, Adam read the instructions by which he would save his life and the kingdom he so loved.

Finis

About the Author

Descended from a long line of storytellers, writers, and savants, Tahir Shah is one of the most prolific authors of his generation. He has published more than sixty books in numerous genres, including travel, fiction, and fantasy, as well as tales for children.

Raised in the tradition of Eastern 'teaching stories', Shah is passionate about stories and storytelling. He regards the ability to learn from folklore as being in us all, what he calls a 'default setting of humankind'. As well as having written scores of books, Shah has made documentaries for National Geographic TV and The History Channel. He is the founder and CEO of the charity, The Scheherazade Foundation.

About the Artist

Maedeh (Mahi) Tajafary was born in Iran. She studied painting and has been working as a professional artist since 2013. Drawing her inspiration from Iran, the lives of its people, and the classic style of Iranian miniatures, Mahi is involved in many artistic projects across the country. She exhibits her work at galleries and festivals in Iran, and has recently begun collaborating with international authors to illustrate their books.

Books By Tahir Shah

The Writer's Craft

The Reason to Write

Workbook: Comprehensive, Volume I & II

Workbook: Fantasy, Volume I & II

Workbook: Fiction, Volume I & II

Workbook: Historical Fiction, Volume I & II

Workbook: Teaching Stories, Volume I & II

Workbook: Travel, Volume I & II

Novels

Jinn Hunter: Book One – The Prism

Jinn Hunter: Book Two – The Jinnslayer

Jinn Hunter: Book Three – The Perplexity

Hannibal Fogg and the Supreme Secret of Man

Casablanca Blues

Eye Spy

Godman

Paris Syndrome

Timbuctoo

Midas

Zigzagzone

Nasrudin

Travels With Nasrudin

The Misadventures of the Mystifying Nasrudin

The Peregrinations of the Perplexing Nasrudin

The Voyages and Vicissitudes of Nasrudin

Nasrudin in the Land of Fools

Travel

Trail of Feathers
Travels With Myself
Beyond the Devil's Teeth
In Search of King Solomon's Mines
House of the Tiger King
In Arabian Nights
The Caliph's House
Sorcerer's Apprentice
Journey Through Namibia

Teaching Stories

The Arabian Nights Adventures
Scorpion Soup
Tales Told to a Melon
The Afghan Notebook
Daydreams of an Octopus & Other Stories
The Caravanserai Stories
Ghoul Brothers
Hourglass
Imaginist
Jinn's Treasure
Jinnlore
Mellified Man
Skeleton Island
Wellspring
When the Sun Forgot to Rise
Outrunning the Reaper
The Cap of Invisibility
On Backgammon Time
The Wondrous Seed

The Paradise Tree
Mouse House
The Hoopoe's Flight
The Old Wind
A Treasury of Tales
The Tale of Double Six
The Forgotten Game
King of the Jinns
The Destiny Ring
Changing the World
Cat, Mouse
Frogland
Mittle-Mittle
Capilongo
The Princess of Zilzilam
The Singing Serpents
The Tale of the Rusty Nail
The Unicorn's Tear
The Clockmaker Who Travelled Through Time
The Fish's Dream
The Man Whose Arms Grew Branches
The Most Foolish of Men
The Shop That Sold Truth
Qwerty
Renaissance
The Man With the Tiger's Head
The Kingdom of Blink
The Wisdom of Celestine
Dream Soup
The Skeleton Factory
An Unexpected Gift

The Problem Exchange
The Pharaoh Code
The Monkey Puzzle Club
Liquid Time
Cat Dog, Dog Cat
Princess Pickle's Laugh

Anthologies
The Anthologies: Africa
The Anthologies: Ceremony
The Anthologies: Childhood
The Anthologies: City
The Anthologies: Danger
The Anthologies: East
The Anthologies: Expedition
The Anthologies: Frontier
The Anthologies: Hinterland
The Anthologies: India
The Anthologies: Jinns
The Anthologies: Jungle
The Anthologies: Magic
The Anthologies: Morocco
The Anthologies: Nasrudin
The Anthologies: People
The Anthologies: Quest
The Anthologies: South
The Anthologies: Taboo
The Anthologies: Teaching Stories
The Clockmaker's Box
The Tahir Shah Fiction Reader
The Tahir Shah Travel Reader

Research

Cultural Research

The Middle East Bedside Book

Three Essays

Edited by

Congress With a Crocodile

A Son of a Son, Volume I

A Son of a Son, Volume II

Screenplays

Casablanca Blues: The Screenplay

Timbuctoo: The Screenplay

A REQUEST

If you enjoyed this book, please review it on your favourite online retailer or review website.

Reviews are an author's best friend.

To stay in touch with Tahir Shah, and to hear about his upcoming releases before anyone else, please sign up for his mailing list:

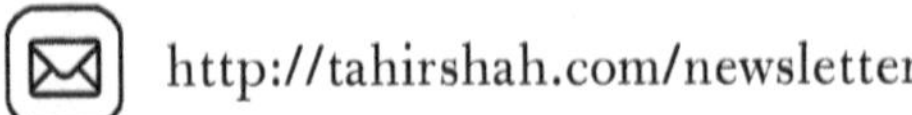

And to follow him on social media, please go to any of the following links:

http://www.twitter.com/humanstew

@tahirshah999

http://www.facebook.com/TahirShahAuthor

http://www.youtube.com/user/tahirshah999

http://www.pinterest.com/tahirshah

https://www.goodreads.com/tahirshahauthor

http://www.tahirshah.com

www.ingramcontent.com/pod-product-compliance
Lightning Source LLC
Chambersburg PA
CBHW030521310726
48979CB00010B/1751/J

* 9 7 8 1 9 1 5 8 7 6 0 5 8 *